Babar characters TM & © 1990 L. de Brunhoff
All rights reserved.
Based on the animated series "Babar"
A Nelvana-Ellipse Presentation
a Nelvana Production in Association with The Clifford Ross Company, Ltd

Based on characters created
by Jean and Laurent de Brunhoff

Image adaptation by Van Gool-Lefevre-Loiseaux
Produced by Twin Books U.K. Ltd, London

This 1990 edition published by JellyBean Press,
distributed by Outlet Book Company, Inc.,
A Random House Company, 225 Park Avenue South,
New York, New York 10003

ISBN 0-517-05214-8

8 7 6 5 4 3 2 1
Printed in Italy

BABAR™

and His Friends

On Vacation

Twin Books

JellyBean Press
New York

It is the first day of summer vacation, and the

children have marked it on the  . Flora

has packed her things for a trip to the seashore–

except for her pet  , which stays home.

The boys are packing their luggage. Alexander says,

"I'm taking my and my cap. But Pom

is mixed up: He thinks it will be snowing at the

beach! Pom, why do you have a 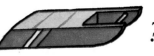 ?"

Arthur is at the window in his explorer's hat,

trying to see the ocean through his  .

"I think we will have a wonderful time," he says.

calendar, turtle, beach ball, sled, binoculars

Babar and Celeste are ready to leave on vacation.

The  is completely packed! In

fact, there is scarcely enough room for everyone.

Where will they put the last  ?

Babar is waiting patiently in the car. He checks

his  and starts the engine. "Now what has

happened to Pom?" asks Celeste with a deep sigh.

She is holding the , so that she can

lock the palace. Finally, Pom comes running down

the stairs. He had almost forgotten his  !

At last, everyone is ready to go!

*car, suitcase,
rearview mirror,
keys,
teddy bear*

As soon as they arrive at the cottage, Pom, Flora,

Arthur, and Alexander decide to go in swimming.

Flora has put on her nicest  , but no

one is paying attention to her when she models it!

"I've found my sand for the beach! " says

Alexander. Pom is so excited that he puts on his

new backward and won't wait while

Arthur blows up his  for him. "Don't

jump around so much, please, Pom," complains

Celeste, who is trying to put on his sailor .

No one notices Rataxes and his wife next door!

bathing suit,
rake,
trunks,
rubber duck,
sailor hat

While Celeste and Babar are unpacking at the

cottage, the children take the big

and go straight to the seashore for their swim.

Alexander puts on his  and walks

carefully into the water. He goes slowly because

his  make him walk like a duck. "The

water is perfect. It's just great!" he says happily.

Suddenly, a  swerves toward Arthur.

To avoid him, Arthur dives directly under a huge

. Just in time. But who is the reckless

windsurfer? It's Rataxes, of course!

beach umbrella,
goggles,
flippers,
windsurfer,
wave

Babar has joined the children on the beach.

"Papa, please show me how to fly my  ,"

asks Alexander. "It's hard to get it into the air."

Arthur and Pom have built a large  .

"It really is a beauty," declares Arthur proudly.

Picking up a sand , he finishes digging the

moat. "Soon we can fill it with water!" Flora is

on her way to them with a brimming .

"Look out!" she calls loudly. "Oh—what a shame!"

Rataxes, in his dark  , didn't see the

castle and walked right over it! He's very sorry.

kite,
sand castle,
spade, pail,
sunglasses

The family has walked down to the harbor.

Arthur wants to climb high up into the  ;

Pom and Alexander would rather play around the

huge old  on the pier. Be careful,

please! Flora has been watching a big

fly overhead. "Look!" she calls. "That bird has

stolen a from the fishermen!"

Side by side, Babar and Celeste are strolling

along the waterfront. They admire the colorful

 that is coming into port. The

fishermen have made a good catch today.

lighthouse,
anchor,
seagull,
fish,
fishing boat

That afternoon, the weather becomes very hot.

Babar sits in a comfortable  to rest.

It's naptime for all the children, who are tired out.

In their , Flora and Pom are asleep

already. Alexander is lying on the grass with his

picture book, propped up on a soft .

Suddenly, he hears a loud splintering sound.

The  Arthur was sitting in has collapsed!

Happily, he doesn't have far to fall and is all right!

Rataxes bursts into laughter behind the 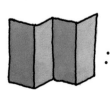 :

He had loosened the bolts on the chair!

rocking chair,
hammock,
cushion,
lounge chair,
screen

One morning, all the children go off fishing.

Pom is lucky: He catches a  with very

big claws. He may need help to get it home!

"Oh, a  !" calls Flora happily. "Isn't it pretty?

And look at this—I've also caught a tiny .

It didn't wiggle out of the net. How funny!"

Alexander teeters on a slippery rock, crying, "I've

just found the biggest in the world!"

Arthur, who hasn't caught anything interesting

in his new 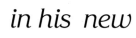 , warns: "Be careful,

Alexander—you could slip on the seaweed."

crab,
starfish,
shrimp,
mussel,
net

Everyone is enjoying an afternoon tennis game.

It's Babar's turn to serve and he sends the

to Arthur, who misses his return shot and complains

"My  is too heavy!"

Flora is in charge of collecting the stray balls.

Alexander has come to the court well prepared;

both the pockets of his  are filled with

extra balls. Celeste has just made a good shot to him

over the  . Pom is wetting down the

dusty court and ends up spraying a spectactor!

The long red  is too slippery for him.

tennis ball,
racket,
shorts, net,
hose

Since their arrival, the children have been asking

to take a trip over to the little  . It isn't

very far away, so Babar gives them permission to

take a small 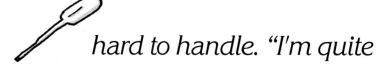 , and they set off.

Alexander can't row as fast as Arthur, because

he finds the big  hard to handle. "I'm quite

sure that pirates buried some treasure here," says

Pom. "Maybe under that  ."

"Oh, look! A shark!" cries Flora, pointing excitedly.

"That's a  ," says Arthur as it comes

closer. "How friendly it is. It's smiling at us."

island,
rowboat,
oar,
palm tree,
dolphin

"Mama, look at the pretty  I found out on

the island," says Flora, back at the cottage.

"I've brought home a ," exclaims Arthur.

"It's prickly, so I wrapped it up in this  !"

Pom has brought back a beautiful piece of colorful

 for Babar, who is busy opening a letter that

has just arrived in the mail. While his father reads

the letter, Alexander looks hopefully at the envelope.

He'd like to get the pink for his collection.

"Listen," says Babar. "The Old Lady and Zephir

have invited us to join them in the mountains!"

seashell,
sea urchin,
towel,
coral,
stamp

The following day, the family is on the road again.

"Children, look at that great  ," says

Celeste enthusiastically. "Isn't it magnificent?"

"How far is it to the Old Lady's  ?"

asks Flora. "I can't wait to see her again."

"I see it now, next to the tall  there," calls

Alexander. "Let's go faster, Papa. Can we pass

that  ? It's going much too slowly."

"No, that wouldn't be very smart," says Babar.

"There's a long  up ahead. Be patient,

please—we're almost there."

mountain,
vacation house,
pine tree,
camper,
tunnel

Everyone is so happy to see old friends again!

"Next time, let's fly up here in a big striped ,"

suggests Pom. "It's much more fun than a car."

Flora has found a and counts the petals.

"Look out!" Arthur calls. "You might be stung by

the that was on that flower!" But Zephir,

who is turning somersaults, reassures them both.

"Oh, no. The bee is going back to its ."

Alexander is sneaking up on a mound of earth to

see a . But the little animal sees him

coming and runs away.

balloon,
daisy,
bee, hive,
woodchuck

All the children have asked if they can camp out,

so Babar sets up a  behind the

house. Flora is going to sleep inside the tent on an

 , with lots of warm blankets. The others

want to sleep out under the stars.

Celeste has given each of them a snug

because nights are chilly in the mountains.

"It's a good thing I brought this  ,"

says Arthur. "Otherwise, I couldn't see a thing."

"This  is wearing me out," complains Zephir.

"But I'm going to catch him. Wait and see!"

tent,
air mattress
sleeping bag,
flashlight,
moth

Celeste has made a delicious picnic lunch, and

everyone has a to drink with it.

"It's fun eating out here in the shade," she says. "But

what a breeze! Babar, quick, your  !"

Hungry Pom has sat down beside the bottle of

 so he can have it all to himself for his hot dog.

Zephir is eating a sandwich half as big as he is!

"That  !" cries Flora suddenly. "It's

moving! And so is yours, Arthur—Look!"

What a surprise: It's a little that has dug

its way out from under the tablecloth!

glass of milk,
napkin,
ketchup,
plate,
mole

A day at the lake keeps everyone busy. Behind

a  , Arthur is learning to water ski.

Babar takes Pom, Alexander, and Zephir out on

a  that glides swiftly across the lake,

as Celeste and the Old Lady watch from the shore.

"Look at Pom waving to us," laughs the Old Lady

gently. "He looks just like a turtle in his 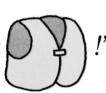 !"

Flora wanders along the shore enjoying the sight of

a  . She would like to pick it, but it is

out of reach. "I know!" she thinks. "If I borrow

the Old Lady's  , I can get it."

motorboat,
sailboat,
life jacket,
water lily,
parasol

Babar is sitting on his portable canvas

beside the river for a peaceful day of fishing.

He has a very good  with a special reel.

But, of course, it is Alexander, with his stick and

string, who catches the day's first  !

"A big trout!" he cries. "How strong it is! Papa,

what should I do now, so I don't lose it?"

Help soon arrives by , as Zephir

and Arthur come to show Alexander how to land

his fish. The Old Lady has her focused:

"We must have a picture as a souvenir."

stool,
fishing rod,
fish,
canoe,
camera

Today, the friends have gone mountain climbing.

Babar is in the lead, with a pick and a  .

For safety's sake, he has roped everyone together.

"Without this  ," grumbles Zephir, "I could

jump from rock to rock all the way up to the top."

"Exactly like that ," laughs Flora.

Alexander is climbing fast—but he stops to see

an  perched on the cliff above him. "He

looks very fierce!" says Alexander. " I don't think

he likes the look of that colorful  .

Maybe he thinks it's another bird."

backpack,
rope,
antelope,
eagle,
hang glider

"I can't believe our vacation is over," says Celeste,

choosing a picture . "Children, let's each get

something to remember our stay in the mountains."

Alexander has found a leather  to buy .

"If I have enough money," he thinks, "I will also get

a for Flora. She likes them so much."

Pom, as usual, wants everything he sees. But

today the fruit baskets filled with fresh

look especially good to him. Babar has picked out

a jar of sweet clover to take home. "It will

remind me of this good mountain air," he says.

postcard,
wallet,
flower,
berries,
honey

The children are helping to clean up before they

leave. Flora wipes the windows with a  .

Alexander, who is proud to be helping, is throwing

everything into a big . But Celeste calls,

"No, not that book! It's brand new, Alexander!"

Pom is busy tickling Zephir with the  . The

little monkey laughs so hard, he loses his balance.

Stepping on the  , he topples over with

the broom and collapses the folding  !

"I do hope things will be a little quieter when we all

get home," sighs Babar.

sponge,
trash can,
feather duster,
scrub brush,
ironing board